HOPSCOTCH

The Best Den Ever

by Anne Cassidy and Deborah Allwright

W
FRANKLIN WATTS
LONDON • SYDNEY

HOPSCOTCH

The Best Den Ever

First published in 2004 by
Franklin Watts
338 Euston Road
London
NW1 3BH

Franklin Watts Australia
Level 17 / 207 Kent Street
Sydney
NSW 2000

A CIP catalogue record for this book is available
from the British Library.

ISBN 978 0 7496 5876 2

Series Editor: Jackie Hamley
Series Advisor: Dr Barrie Wade
Cover Design: Jason Anscomb
Design: Peter Scoulding

Printed in China

Franklin Watts is a division of
Hachette Children's Books,
an Hachette Livre UK company.

Sam wanted to build a den.

His sister Sophie wanted to help.

"Let's build our den in the garden,"
said Sam. He got some deck chairs
and an umbrella.

"We can use these sheets," he said.
Sam and Sophie made a den
under the deck chairs.

Inside the den, Sam put cushions, toys and a chair for Sophie.

home
sweet
home

Sam's brother, Joe, came to see it.
"Look!" cried Sam. "We've finished
building our den!"

"This is the worst den ever," said Joe. "It'll fall down! Look at those silly sheets and shaky deck chairs!" "They're OK!" said Sam.

Sam tied the sheets tighter and
fixed the deck chairs.
"Well, the umbrella is full
of holes!" said Joe.

Later it rained. The umbrella leaked. The deck chairs got soaked. The sheets fell down.

"Oh no!" cried Sam. He picked up
the cushions and ran. Sophie
pulled her teddy bear behind her.

When the sun came out,
Sam tried again. "This time
we'll build our den under
this tree," he said.
"And this time it
won't fall down!"

Sophie helped to make a pile of
bricks. Sam fetched some wood.

On the top they laid some towels.

"That's much better!" said Sam.

Inside the den, Sam put a chair, a table, some cups, a tray with biscuits and a drink for Sophie.

"I could build a much better den," said Joe. "And it wouldn't fall over!"

"This den won't fall over!" said Sam.

But later it was windy. The towels blew away. The wood fell over.

"Quick! Let's go!" said Sam.

"I told you it would fall over!"
said Joe, laughing.

"We need to find a better place
to build our den," said Sam.
They looked around.

Sophie's room was too small.

Sam's room was too messy!

Sam and Sophie looked everywhere.

The kitchen was too full.

The living room was too tidy.

The hallway was too empty.

Suddenly Sam had an idea.
"I know a good place!"
he whispered to Sophie.

Sam got some pillows and blankets.

He found a chair and a stool.

Sophie brought toys from her room.

They made the best den ever ...

... in Joe's room!

"WHAT'S THIS?" demanded Joe.

"It's the best den ever!" said Sam.

"Well, I suppose it's not too bad!"

laughed Joe.

Hopscotch has been specially designed to fit the requirements of the National Literacy Strategy. It offers real books by top authors and illustrators for children developing their reading skills. There are 49 Hopscotch stories to choose from:

Marvin, the Blue Pig
ISBN 978 0 7496 4619 6

Plip and Plop
ISBN 978 0 7496 4620 2

The Queen's Dragon
ISBN 978 0 7496 4618 9

Flora McQuack
ISBN 978 0 7496 4621 9

Willie the Whale
ISBN 978 0 7496 4623 3

Naughty Nancy
ISBN 978 0 7496 4622 6

Run!
ISBN 978 0 7496 4705 6

The Playground Snake
ISBN 978 0 7496 4706 3

"Sausages!"
ISBN 978 0 7496 4707 0

Bear in Town
ISBN 978 0 7496 5875 5

Pippin's Big Jump
ISBN 978 0 7496 4710 0

Whose Birthday Is It?
ISBN 978 0 7496 4709 4

The Princess and the Frog
ISBN 978 0 7496 5129 9

Flynn Flies High
ISBN 978 0 7496 5130 5

Clever Cat
ISBN 978 0 7496 5131 2

Moo!
ISBN 978 0 7496 5332 3

Izzie's Idea
ISBN 978 0 7496 5334 7

Roly-poly Rice Ball
ISBN 978 0 7496 5333 0

I Can't Stand It!
ISBN 978 0 7496 5765 9

Cockerel's Big Egg
ISBN 978 0 7496 5767 3

How to Teach a Dragon Manners
ISBN 978 0 7496 5873 1

The Truth about those Billy Goats
ISBN 978 0 7496 5766 6

Marlowe's Mum and the Tree House
ISBN 978 0 7496 5874 8

The Truth about Hansel and Gretel
ISBN 978 0 7496 4708 7

The Best Den Ever
ISBN 978 0 7496 5876 2

ADVENTURE STORIES

Aladdin and the Lamp
ISBN 978 0 7496 6692 7

Blackbeard the Pirate
ISBN 978 0 7496 6690 3

George and the Dragon
ISBN 978 0 7496 6691 0

Jack the Giant-Killer
ISBN 978 0 7496 6693 4

TALES OF KING ARTHUR

1. The Sword in the Stone
ISBN 978 0 7496 6694 1

2. Arthur the King
ISBN 978 0 7496 6695 8

3. The Round Table
ISBN 978 0 7496 6697 2

4. Sir Lancelot and the Ice Castle
ISBN 978 0 7496 6698 9

TALES OF ROBIN HOOD

Robin and the Knight
ISBN 978 0 7496 6699 6

Robin and the Monk
ISBN 978 0 7496 6700 9

Robin and the Silver Arrow
ISBN 978 0 7496 6703 0

Robin and the Friar
ISBN 978 0 7496 6702 3

FAIRY TALES

The Emperor's New Clothes
ISBN 978 0 7496 7421 2

Cinderella
ISBN 978 0 7496 7417 5

Snow White
ISBN 978 0 7496 7418 2

Jack and the Beanstalk
ISBN 978 0 7496 7422 9

The Three Billy Goats Gruff
ISBN 978 0 7496 7420 5

The Pied Piper of Hamelin
ISBN 978 0 7496 7419 9

HISTORIES

Toby and the Great Fire of London
ISBN 978 0 7496 7079 5 *
ISBN 978 0 7496 7410 6

Pocahontas the Peacemaker
ISBN 978 0 7496 7080 1 *
ISBN 978 0 7496 7411 3

Grandma's Seaside Bloomers
ISBN 978 0 7496 7081 8 *
ISBN 978 0 7496 7412 0

Hoorah for Mary Seacole
ISBN 978 0 7496 7082 5 *
ISBN 978 0 7496 7413 7

Remember the 5th of November
ISBN 978 0 7496 7083 2 *
ISBN 978 0 7496 7414 4

Tutankhamun and the Golden Chariot
ISBN 978 0 7496 7084 9 *
ISBN 978 0 7496 7415 1

* hardback